I AM MY ANCESTORS DREAMS COME TRUE!

P9-CRX-108

SAVE OUR PLANE

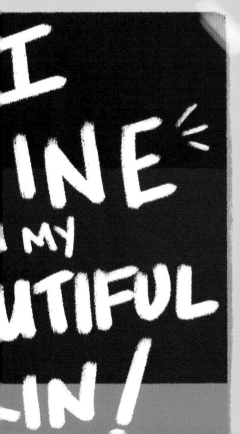

I
INE
MY
UTIFUL
IN!

WATER IS LIFE

THIS BOOK WAS
WRITTEN IN OUR HOMES
ON THE
UNCEDED TERRITORY
OF THE
CHOCHENYO OHLONE PEOPLE

WHERE ARE YOU IN THE WORLD?

WHOSE LAND
ARE YOU ON?

YOU ARE NOT ALONE

WORDS BY TWO-TIME GRAMMY NOMINEES

ALPHABET ROCKERS

PICTURES BY

ASHLEY EVANS

WHEN YOU READ THIS BOOK, YOU'LL MEET KIDS JUST LIKE YOU. KIDS WHO ARE PROUD OF WHO THEY ARE. KIDS WHO WANT TO BELONG, WHO WANT TO STAND UP. KIDS WHO ARE MAKING THE WORLD BEAUTIFUL BY BEING TRUE TO THEMSELVES.

WE WANT TO HEAR YOUR VOICE TOO.

AT THE END OF EACH KID'S STORY, SAY IT OUT LOUD,

"YOU ARE NOT ALONE!"

LET THEM KNOW THAT YOU REALLY GOT THEIR BACK.

sourcebooks
eXplore

ARE YOU READY TO GO?

Before we do,

I want you to know something.

YOU DON'T KNOW ME,

but I bet you see the sun rise

and set like I do.

YOU DON'T KNOW ME,

but when I see a star in the sky,

I SEE MAGIC.

YOU DON'T KNOW ME,

but I wonder if you look at your

skin the way I look at mine.

You don't know me,

but I need you to know that

I don't always feel safe here.

AND I DON'T KNOW YOU,
but I hope you never have
to feel that way.

If you really knew me,

when you'd see me you would think:

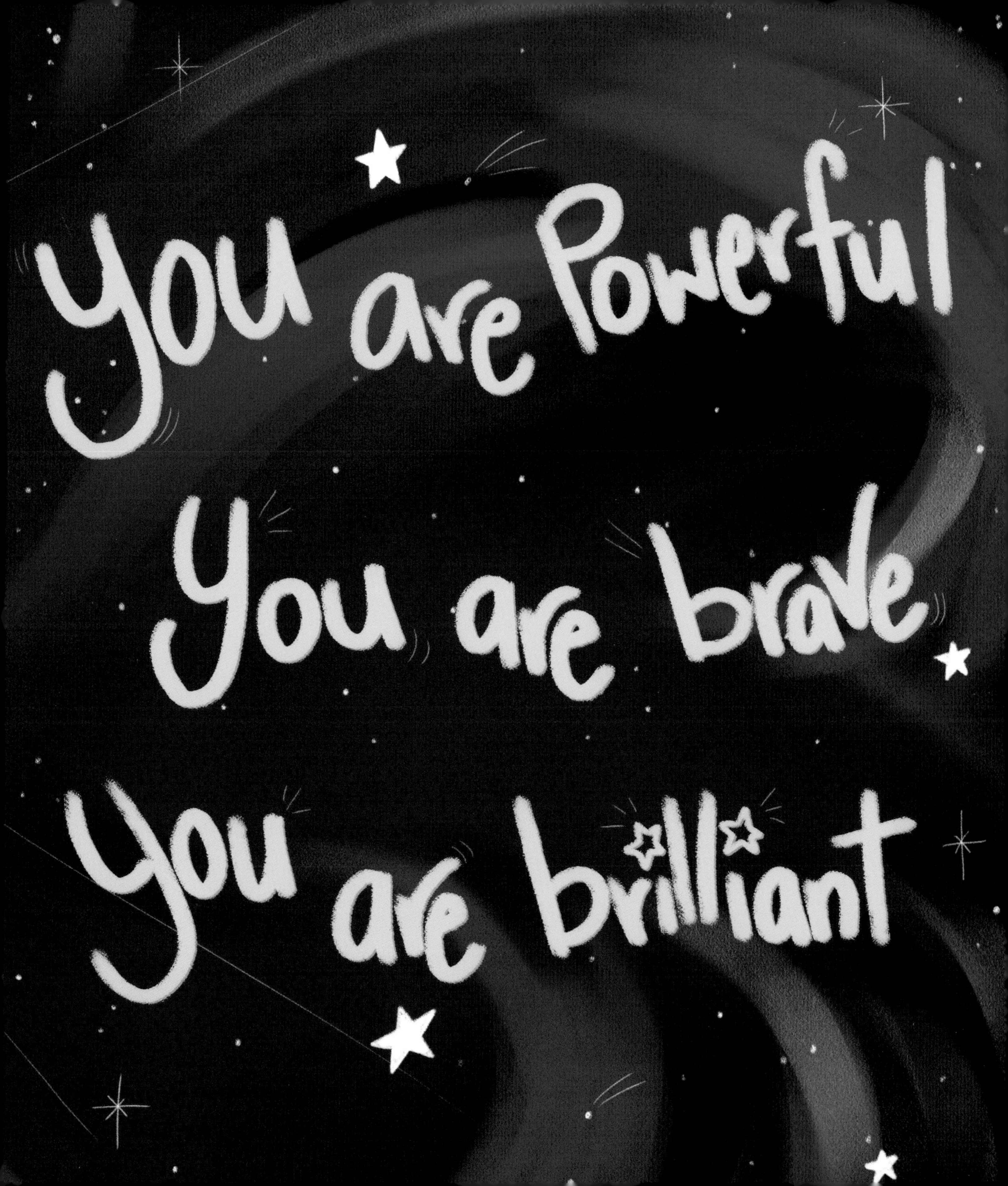

You are Powerful

You are brave

You are brilliant

But you don't know me yet,

so I can only imagine what you think by looking at me.

Today, I want you to really **SEE ME.**

Are you ready now?

Let's go.

YOU ARE NOT ALONE.

I'M READY!

Have you ever felt like people didn't get you?

I have. MANY TIMES.

No one says my name right at school.

Can't pronounce it,

and sometimes even after they say my name,

they make a face.

It's not that hard to say
my name, promise.
Makes me feel like school
wasn't built for me.
I'm supposed to be there to learn,
but no one is learning
how to see ME.

Except for my friend.

He always gets my name right.

He even corrects people when they get it wrong.

That makes me feel safe. At home. Like I belong.

Bet you could work at it too.

Let's take a deep breath. I need one. In...out.

Maybe one more.

Have you ever felt like you couldn't share your real feelings?

I need you to know that we all have big feelings.

Even me.

We're all going through something at some time or another.

So there's a lot of reasons why our feelings get so big, right?

The thing is, I don't always feel safe to share my feelings.

AND I GOT TO FEEL THEM.

When I say I'm hurt, do you feel my pain?

When I say something is unfair to me,

but you say it's fair for you, what does that make it?

When I meditate, it all gets clear.

And if you listen, you will really hear.

YOU ARE NOT ALONE.
YOU ARE ENOUGH.

Did you hear that?

Yea, that's my song. I MADE iT.

I am my destiny—connecting history, cultures,

languages, and family in every remix.

See, I'm a DJ.

I'm making music that sends a signal to kids everywhere that there is no limit to being you. You are so many things.

I am so many things. We're all stardust, and this is our sky, our song, our world.

DO YOU HEAR iT? DO YOU FEEL ME?
YOU ARE NOT ALONE.
I HEAR YOU.

This song... It's taking me out of this world.

Where I see the sky.

The whole GALAXY.

YOU ARE NOT ALONE

It's just...so...me. It's magical. It's like I'm a new constellation.

And I like it up here. It's like I just spilled rice on the floor in the

messiest perfect pattern.

Bet the world knows now I've always been here. Shining.

YOU SEE ALL THE STARS THAT I AM?

"YOU ARE NOT ALONE. I SEE YOU!"

When I look up at the sky, I see my people.

I'm larger than this page,

than this land,

than even words.

WE'RE THAT POWERFUL.

See, I'm from the lineage of

the first people of this land.

And when I help the community,

I MAKE THE PLANET BETTER FOR SEVEN GENERATIONS TO COME.

I'm from a lineage of advocates and dreamers.
I SEE YOU FOR YOU.
I LOVE YOU FOR YOU
and will **STAND UP WITH**
and **FOR YOU.**

I AM MY ANCESTORS DREAMS COME TRUE!

YOU ARE NOT ALONE

We've seen the statues crumble, that's a start.

So I'll tell you this, I want you to know **MY STORY.**

People and history books have tried to share it for me.

But share my story, that way history won't erase my story.

Know that I don't want to do this alone.

I WANT YOU TO STAND UP WITH ME.

Can I trust that you will remember you are on my community's land?

"YOU'RE NOT ALONE. I'LL STAND UP WITH YOU. I WILL REMEMBER."

I WANT YOU TO ASK ME.

But I don't like some of the questions.

Maybe you don't know which questions feel like friendship,

and which ones feel like "ouch."

If you get a feeling inside you

like your question might sting,

let it go.

Don't share it with me.

NOT ALL THOUGHTS NEED TO BECOME WORDS IN THE WORLD.

I have a friend who loves me for me.

Doesn't ask about my body parts,

but does want to know what

it is like being nonbinary.

Checks in with me when the teachers

get jammed up on my pronouns.

Offers to go shopping with me

for school clothes...

SO I AM NOT ALONE.

My friend holds my truth,

and stands up with me.

They're cool with me being

EXACTLY WHO I AM,

IN ALL THE WAYS.

Can you get on board with us for the ride?

"YOU ARE NOT ALONE. I'LL GO WITH YOU."

THIS IS THE STORY:

You and me. See?

**YOUR HiSTORY,
MY HiSTORY,
THEiR HiSTORY.**

We learn them together.

**I AM ME BECAUSE
YOU ARE YOU.**

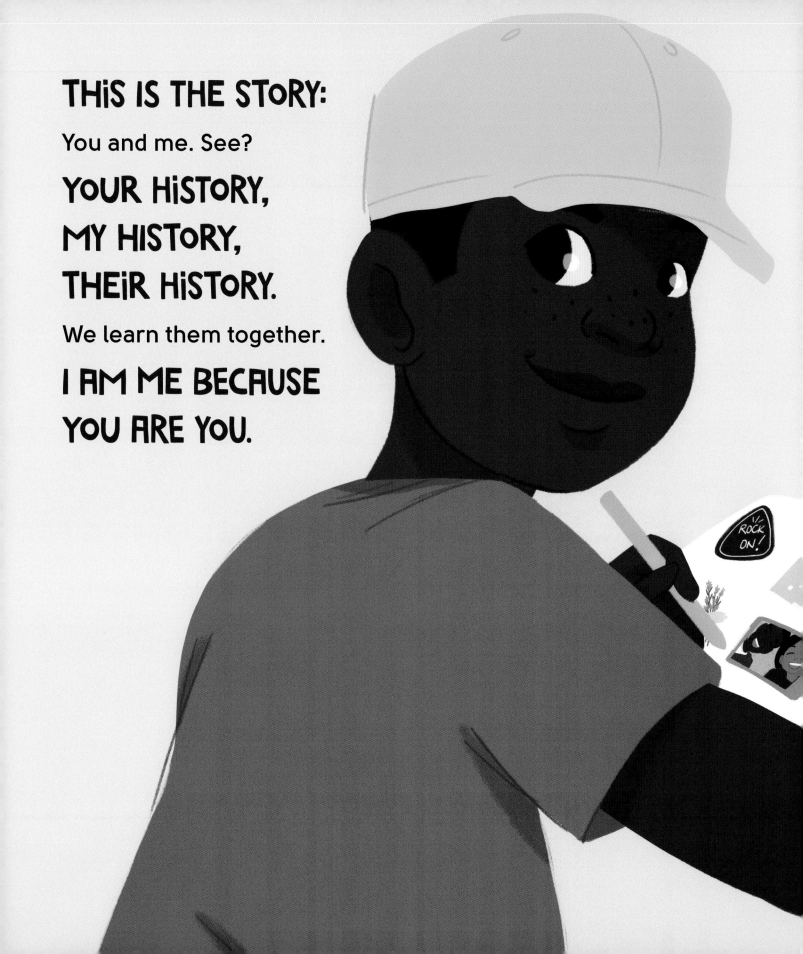

YOUR STORY MATTERS, and you know what?

I want to read and write your story with all the colors of the universe that are in you.

SO I NEED TO HEAR YOU.

Your ideas...

what you see in the world that echoes your brave heart.

Where do you find your story in the lights of the world?

Is it in the one night star that burns through the city skyline,

always here for us?

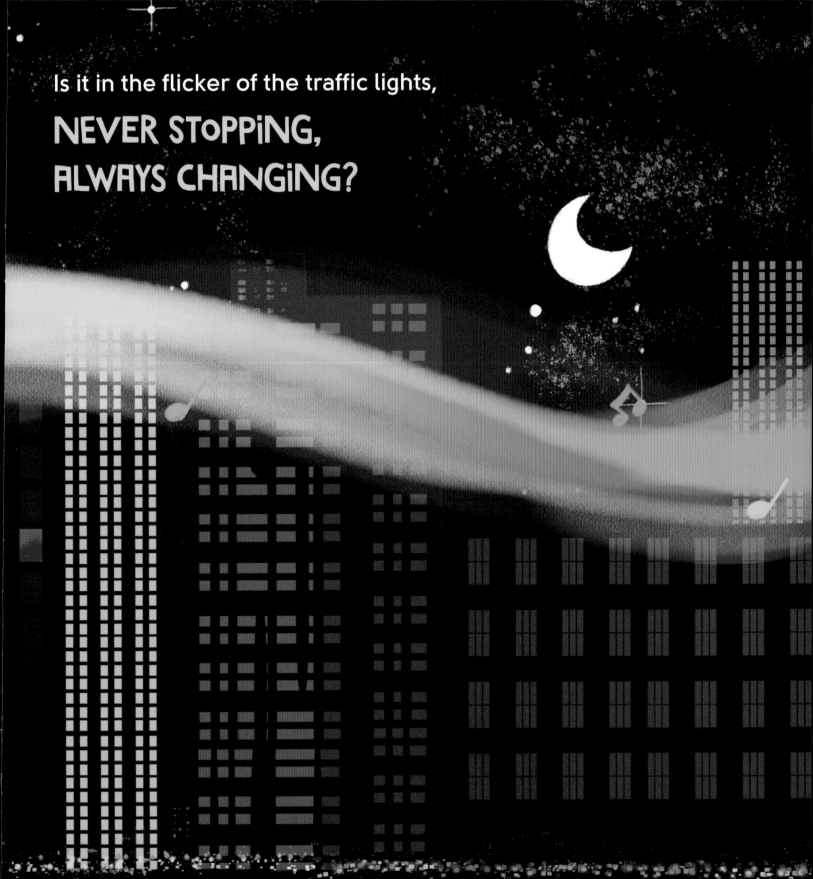

Is it in the flicker of the traffic lights,

NEVER STOPPING,
ALWAYS CHANGING?

Is it in the sunlight that blocks everything out when it bounces off yesterday's puddle and pools in our eyes?

If what you see first is a rainbow,

I hope I can be in the colors with you.

I HOPE YOU ALWAYS KNOW
YOU ARE NOT ALONE.

Can you press pause for a second?

It's going too fast!

BREATHE.

I want to remember

this moment.

ME AND YOU. TOGETHER.

BELIEVING.

WISHING.

LISTENING.

This is special.

WE ARE
NOT ALONE.

Can this be the rest

of the story?

If you feel it in your heart and you're ready to take part,

say I'm not alone—I'M NOT ALONE.

If you feel it your soul and you're ready to roll,

say you're not alone—YOU'RE NOT ALONE.

If you feel it in your gut and you're ready to step up,

say we're not alone—WE'RE NOT ALONE

I'M NOT ALONE—YOU'RE NOT ALONE—WE'RE NOT ALONE.

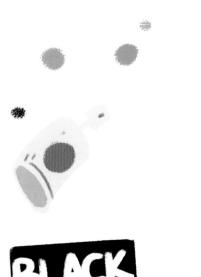

WHEN I DON'T SEE MYSELF ON THE PAGES OF A BOOK...

Where is my story?

I don't see myself in this book.

The kids don't look exactly like me.

Their experiences aren't like mine.

I wish that I could see myself here too.

I want to see my story

and my community's in books.

Does it still need to be written?

STORIES ARE IMPORTANT.

We want to hear your voice, echo your pain,

celebrate your triumph, and rewrite the world with you.

If all you have is a pen, use it.

If all you have is a song, sing it.

If all you have is a drum, play it.

GET LOUD.

You and your community deserve to be seen,

heard and understood.

And why not you, to share your voice?

Let other kids know they're not alone.

ABOUT ALPHABET ROCKERS

ALPHABET ROCKERS make music that makes change. Led by Kaitlin McGaw and Tommy Shepherd, they create brave spaces to shape a more equitable world through hip-hop, as two-time GRAMMY-nominees, Othering & Belonging Institute Fellows, and industry leaders for change. They work in partnership with the community to create media that reflects the culture of belonging they want to see in the world. Reaching over three million families since 2007, Alphabet Rockers inspire American kids and families to stand up to hate and be their brave and beautiful selves.

ALPHABET ROCKERS Co-FOUNDERS

KAITLIN MCGAW (she/her) is a writer, listener, and artist based in Oakland, CA, on Ohlone lands. Her path in anti-racism and art began as a high school student in Belmont, MA, where community dialogue, activism, and poetry framed her purpose and relationship with the world. Kaitlin is a graduate of Harvard University with a BA in Afro-American Studies. She is also a two-time GRAMMY nominee, an artist fellow, and a deeply committed partner for change, often stepping back for others to shine, and stepping up for truth and our collective humanity. Kaitlin believes radical imagination begins with the way we read, sing, and ask questions of the world with our children. She is the mother of two creative children of her own, whom she is raising with her husband Adhi.

TOMMY SOULATI SHEPHERD (he/him/they) is an internationally renowned actor, playwright, composer, educator, rapper, drummer, beatboxer, and music producer. Tommy (aka Emcee Soulati) is a long-time member of the performance group Campo Santo who continue to tell stories of the people and Oakland's own Antique Naked Soul—The Soundtrack for Revolution. Tommy has composed, performed, and toured internationally with Marc Bamuthi Joseph, collaborating on Scourge; the break/s; Spoken World; red, black and GREEN: a blues; and /peh-LO-tah/. Tommy won a 2018 Isadora Duncan Award for his composition work and is a two-time GRAMMY nominee. Tommy brings love for family, art, activism, and community building to all of his work. His inspiration and hope for a more joyful and equitable world is felt through the hearts of families everywhere.

ABOUT THE ILLUSTRATOR

ASHLEY EVANS is an artist and illustrator with a focus on digital art. It all started when she picked up a crayon as a kid and she hasn't stopped drawing since. Ashley's work is colorful, character-driven, eclectic, and usually covered in stars! Originally from Queens, NY, she now stays in North Carolina. When she's not drawing, you can find her on mom duty, reading an ever growing stack of books, or baking something sweet.

For Adhi, Kiran, and Jasmine, whose names hold our family history and whose imagination lights my heart.

May you never feel alone in who you are.

KAITLIN MCGAW

I dedicate this book to Anna, Tommy III, Sawyer, and the entire Shepherd/Luera Family.

Thank you for holding me up and holding it down!

TOMMY SOULATI SHEPHERD

For everyone who has ever felt their voice or effort wasn't enough.

Your voice and vision have power and you are never alone.

ASHLEY EVANS

Text © 2022 by Alphabet Rockers
Illustrations © 2022 by Ashley Evans
Cover and internal design by Jordan Kost/Sourcebooks
Cover and internal design © 2022 by Sourcebooks

Sourcebooks and the colophon are registered trademarks of Sourcebooks.

The characters and events portrayed in this book are fictitious or are used fictitiously.
Any similarity to real persons, living or dead, is purely coincidental and not intended by the author.

The full color art was created in Photoshop with a Wacom Cintiq tablet.

Published by Sourcebooks eXplore, an imprint of Sourcebooks Kids
P.O. Box 4410, Naperville, Illinois 60567-4410
(630) 961-3900
sourcebookskids.com

Library of Congress Cataloging-in-Publication Data is on file with the publisher.

Source of Production: Phoenix Color, Hagerstown, Maryland, USA
Date of Production: October 2021
Run Number: 5022847

Printed and bound in the United States of America.
PHC 10 9 8 7 6 5 4 3 2 1